A New True Book

BASEBALL

By Ray Broekel

This "true book" was prepared
under the direction of
Illa Podendorf,
formerly with the Laboratory School,
University of Chicago

CHILDRENS PRESS, CHICAGO

PHOTO CREDITS

Ray DeAragon—10, 13 (left), 17 (left), 20, 24, 25, 27 (right), 30 (right), 34 (2 photos), 38 (2 photos), 40 (right), 43 (bottom left and right), 44 Bottom

G. Robarge—2, 14, 18

Robert B. Shaver—17 (right), 40 (left)

Steve Schwartz—23

Howard Zryb—37 (left and right)

George Gojkovich—37 (center)

Al Schaefer—4, 8, 13 (right), 27 (left), 29, 43 (top left)

Candee & Associates—16

Lynn M. Stone—22, 33

Tony Freeman—Cover, 6 (bottom), 44 (top)

Clifton Boutelle—30 (left)

Los Angeles Dodgers photo—15

Cover—Little league baseball game

Library of Congress Cataloging in Publication Data

Broekel, Ray.
   Baseball.

   (A New true book)
   Cover title: The true book of baseball.
   Summary: Describes briefly all aspects of baseball including the object of the game, the field, the equipment, positions, plays, teams, leagues, famous players, and games.
   1. Baseball—Juvenile literature. [1. Base-ball] I. Title. II. Title: The true book of baseball.
GV867.5.B76   796.357'2   81-38480
ISBN 0-516-01616-4   AACR2

New 1983 Edition

Copyright© 1982 by Regensteiner Publishing Enterprises, Inc.
All rights reserved. Published simultaneously in Canada.
Printed in the United States of America.
    9 10 R 91 90 89

TABLE OF CONTENTS

The Game of Baseball . . . 5

Amateur Baseball . . . 7

Pro Baseball . . . 8

Team Uniforms . . . 11

Things the Players Use . . . 12

The Playing Field . . . 15

Pitcher and Catcher . . . 17

The Infielders . . . 19

The Outfielders . . . 21

The Umpire . . . 23

Innings . . . 25

Hits and Outs . . . 27

Strikes and Balls . . . 29

Batters . . . 32

Base Runners . . . 35

National League Teams . . . 36

American League Teams . . . 39

The World Series . . . 42

The Fun of Baseball . . . 45

Words You Should Know . . . 46

Index . . . 47

Playing in the little leagues

THE GAME OF BASEBALL

"Play ball!" the umpire shouts.

Another baseball game has started.

A baseball game is played between two teams. The teams take turns batting and playing in the field. The team in the field tries to stop the other team from scoring.

Watching or playing baseball is fun.

AMATEUR BASEBALL

Some players play baseball just for fun. They are called amateurs.

Boys and girls are amateurs. So are many grown-up players.

Some amateurs play on teams.

Most teams play in a league. Teams in leagues play each other.

Professional baseball

PRO BASEBALL

Some players get paid to play baseball. They are called professionals, or pros.

There are many professional leagues.

Most players start playing pro ball in minor leagues in North America.

Players in the minor leagues often hope to go to major league teams.

The best pro players are in the major leagues.

There are two major leagues. They are the National League and the American League.

TEAM UNIFORMS

Pro players wear a baseball uniform.

The uniform is a shirt, pants, socks, a cap, and baseball shoes.

The team name is often on the front of the shirt. Numbers are on the back. Sometimes, names of the players are on the backs of their shirts.

THINGS THE PLAYERS USE

Each player uses a glove. Gloves are also called mitts.

A catcher uses a catcher's mitt.

A first baseman uses a first baseman's mitt.

Other players use mitts called fielder's gloves.

Mitts help players catch
the ball. There is padding
on the mitts. It keeps
players' hands from getting
hurt.

Bats are of different lengths. Some kinds are heavier than others.

But baseballs are all the same. They are all the same size. They all weigh the same.

They are small and hard.

THE PLAYING FIELD

A baseball playing field is called a diamond.

The diamond has four bases. There are 90 feet between each of the bases.

There is also an outfield.
It is a big area behind the
diamond.

Beginning players play
on a smaller diamond.

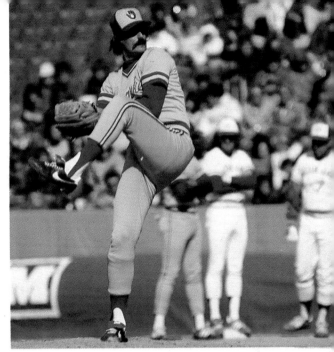

PITCHER AND CATCHER

The pitcher throws from the pitcher's mound. The pitcher's job is to get each batter out.

Most pitchers are righthanded.

Some pitchers are lefthanded. They are called lefties, or southpaws.

A pitcher throws to a catcher behind home plate.

The catcher wears a mask and other things to protect himself.

A runner is trying to score. The catcher took his mask off to make it easier to see the ball.

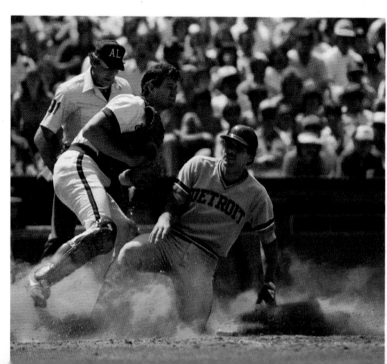

THE INFIELDERS

The infielders try to stop a ball that is hit. They try to tag base runners out.

The first baseman plays near first base.

The third baseman plays near third base.

The second baseman plays near second base.

The shortstop plays
between second and third
base.

The infielders work
together to get base
runners out.

THE OUTFIELDERS

There are three outfielders. They try to catch balls that are hit to the outfield. They throw the ball to infielders to get base runners out.

The left fielder plays out between third and second base.

The center fielder plays
out behind second base.
The right fielder plays
out between second and
first base.

THE UMPIRE

Umpires judge a baseball game. They are not on any team.

They tell when a pitch is a strike. They tell when it is a ball.

They tell if a ball is a
hit.

They tell when players
make outs.

There are often four
umpires for each game.

INNINGS

Pro baseball games are
nine innings long.

Each team gets to bat in
each inning. The team
stays at bat until three
outs are made.

Outs can be made many ways. A batter can strike out. He can fly out or ground out. A batter can be tagged by an infielder while he is a base runner.

The team with the most runs at the end of the game is the winner.

HITS AND OUTS

A team must score runs to win games. So each player bats. When the ball is hit, the batter runs to the bases.

If the batter runs as far as first base, it is a single.

If the runner gets to second base, it is a double.

If the runner goes to third base, it is a triple.

A home run means the batter can run all around the bases. A run is scored.

An out happens when a player tries to get to a base but cannot.

STRIKES AND BALLS

Pitchers do not want the other team to hit the ball. They try to make the other team miss the ball.

Pitchers throw strikes. It
is a strike when the batter
swings and misses the
ball. It is a strike when the
batter doesn't swing, but
the pitch is good.

Three strikes make an
out.

Sometimes a pitch is not good. It may be too high or too low. It may be too close or too far away from the batter. Then the pitch is called a ball.

Four balls mean a walk. The batter goes to first base with a walk.

There is an umpire behind home plate. He tells if a pitch is a ball or a strike.

BATTERS

The batter tries to get on base.

One way to get on base is to get a hit. Another way is to get a walk. Players also get on base if a player on the other team makes an error.

Some players bat right-handed. Others bat left-handed. Some can bat either way.

Batters wear hard hats
to protect them when they
bat.

BASE RUNNERS

When a batter gets on base, he is a base runner.

Base runners try to move from one base to another. They run when another batter hits the ball.

Base runners can also try to steal bases.

Each time a base runner crosses home plate, a run is scored.

NATIONAL LEAGUE
TEAMS

There are twelve National League teams. Six play in the East Division. Six are in the West Division.

"Bake" McBride,
Philadelphia Phillies

Bill Buckner,
Chicago Cubs

Darrell Porter,
St. Louis Cardinals

East Division

- Chicago Cubs
- Montreal Expos
- New York Mets
- Philadelphia Phillies
- Pittsburgh Pirates
- St. Louis Cardinals

Steve Yeager,
Los Angeles Dodgers

Tom Seaver,
Cincinnati Reds

West Division

- Atlanta Braves
- Cincinnati Reds
- Houston Astros
- Los Angeles Dodgers
- San Diego Padres
- San Francisco Giants

AMERICAN LEAGUE TEAMS

There are fourteen American League teams. Seven play in the East Division. Seven are in the West Division.

Dave Winfield,
New York Yankees

Alan Trammell,
Detroit Tigers

East Division

- Baltimore Orioles
- Boston Red Sox
- Cleveland Indians
- Detroit Tigers
- Milwaukee Brewers
- New York Yankees
- Toronto Blue Jays

West Division

- California Angels
- Chicago White Sox
- Kansas City Royals
- Minnesota Twins
- Oakland Athletics
- Seattle Mariners
- Texas Rangers

Do any of these teams play near where you live?

THE WORLD SERIES

The best team in each league wins the pennant. That team is champion of its league.

The National League champions then play the American League champions. That is called the World Series.

Above: Ernie Banks and Billy Williams both played for the Chicago Cubs. Ernie Banks, now in the Hall of Fame, is called "Mr. Cub." Many people thought Billy Williams had the best swing of his time.

Above: Hank Aaron, also in the Hall of Fame, throws out the first ball in the 1973 World Series.

Bottom left: The 1974 World Series was played between the Oakland A's and the Los Angeles Dodgers.

In the World Series a team must win four games. Then they are that year's World Champion team.

THE FUN OF BASEBALL

Watching a baseball game can be fun.

You can cheer when your favorite player gets a hit.

Playing baseball is fun, too. You can cheer for your own team. And they can cheer for you.

WORDS YOU SHOULD KNOW

amateur(AM • ah • cher) — a person who does something just for
    fun and does not get paid

ball(BAWL) — a pitch that is not good; a pitch that is not thrown into
    the strike range.

champion(CHAMP • yun) — the winner

diamond(DYE • mund) — that part of a baseball field that makes up
    the infield.

error(AIR • er) — mistake.

favorite(FAIV • er • it) — liked best

fly out — a batted ball that is caught by a fielder before it hits the
    ground

ground out — a batted ball that is caught as it bounces or rolls on
    the ground and thrown to a base player before the
    batter gets there

hit — a batted ball that is hit so that the batter can get on base

infield(IN • feeld) — the part of a baseball field that is made up of
    the four bases

inning(IN • ing) — the part of a baseball game in which each team
    comes to bat

judge(JUJ) — to rule

league(LEEG) — a group of sport teams

major league(MAY • jer • LEEG) — the most important group of
    baseball teams

minor league(MY • ner LEEG) — the less important group of
    baseball teams

mound — small hill on which a baseball pitcher stands

outfield(OUT • feeld) — that part of a baseball field beyond the
    bases

pennant(PEN • ent) — a flag that means a team is the champion of
    a league

professional(pro • FESH • un • el) — one who is paid for doing
    something that others do for fun

score(SKORE)—to get a player around the four bases for a run

southpaw(SOUTH • paw)—a pitcher who throws the ball with the left hand

steal(STEEL)—to run to another base without the ball being batted

strike out—to get a batter out with three strikes

umpire(UM • pyre)—a person who rules on the plays

uniform(YOO • nih • form)—clothes that are worn when playing baseball

walk(WAWK)—to let a batter get to first base because the pitcher threw four balls

INDEX

amateur baseball, 7

American League, 9, 39-41, 42

Atlanta Braves, 38

balls (umpire's call), 23, 24, 31

Baltimore Orioles, 40

baseballs, 14

base runners, 19, 20, 21, 26, 28, 35

bases, 15, 19, 20, 21, 22, 27, 28, 31, 32, 35

bats, 14

batters, 17, 26, 27, 28, 30, 31, 32, 33, 35

Boston Red Sox, 40

California Angels, 41

catchers, 18

catcher's mask, 18

catcher's mitt, 12

center fielder, 22

Chicago Cubs, 37

Chicago White Sox, 41

Cincinnati Reds, 38

Cleveland Indians, 40

Detroit Tigers, 40

diamond, 15, 16

doubles, 28

East Division, American League, 39, 40

East Division, National League, 36, 37

errors, 32

fielder's gloves, 12

first base, 19, 22, 28, 31

first baseman, 19

first baseman's mitt, 12

fun of baseball, 45

gloves, 12
hits, 24, 32
home plate, 18, 31, 35
home runs, 28
Houston Astros, 38
infielders, 19, 20, 21, 26
innings, 25
Kansas City Royals, 41
leagues, 7, 8
left fielder, 21
Los Angeles Dodgers, 38
major leagues, 9
Milwaukee Brewers, 40
Minnesota Twins, 41
minor leagues, 9
mitts, 12, 13
Montreal Expos, 37
National League, 9, 36-38, 42
New York Mets, 37
New York Yankees, 40
Oakland Athletics, 41
outfield, 16, 21
outfielders, 21, 22
outs, 24, 25, 26, 28, 30
pennant, 42
Philadelphia Phillies, 37
pitchers, 17, 18, 29, 30
pitcher's mound, 17
Pittsburgh Pirates, 37

playing field, 15, 16
professional baseball, 8, 9
right fielder, 22
runs, 26, 28, 35
St. Louis Cardinals, 37
San Diego Padres, 38
San Francisco Giants, 38
Seattle Mariners, 41
second base, 19, 20, 21, 22, 28
second baseman, 19
shortstop, 20
singles, 28
southpaws, 18
stealing bases, 35
strikes, 23, 26, 30, 31
teams, 5, 7, 9, 25, 26, 27, 36-43
Texas Rangers, 41
third base, 19, 20, 21, 28
third baseman, 19
Toronto Blue Jays, 40
triples, 28
umpires, 5, 23, 24, 31
uniforms, 11
walks, 31, 32
West Division, American League,
  39, 41
West Division, National League,
  36, 38
World Champion team, 43
World Series, 42, 43

About the author

*Ray Broekel is a full-time freelance writer who lives with his wife,
Peg, and a dog, Fergus, in Ipswich, Massachusetts. He has had
twenty years of experience as a children's book editor and
newspaper supervisor, and has taught many subjects in
kindergarten through college levels. Dr. Broekel has had over
1,000 stories and articles published, and over 100 books. His first
book was published in 1956 by Childrens Press.*